Text and Illustrations Copyright © 2015 by Schertevear Q. Watkins
Address all inquiries to:
Baobab Books
Email: bbfbooks@gmail.com

ISBN-13:
978-0692553923 (Baobab Publishing)

ISBN-10:
0692553924

Author Bio

Schertevear Q. Watkins is a former educator and divorced mother of two. Her love for teaching is her inspiration for writing Children's Literature.

Schertevear's goal is to bring positive influences into the lives of as many children as possible through her characters. Schertevear writes books that promote learning, character development, social skills, family and more.

FAIRYTALE ENDINGS

Fairytale Endings is a unique Fairytale Series with modern stories and diverse characters from various ethnicities, cultures, countries or with other unique characteristics. Although these stories may often capture something from the main character's heritage or background, these stories will all be up to date and engaging, to capture the interest of all children.

THIS BOOK BELONGS TO

Once there was a little girl named Hope who lived in a large house with lots of space to roam and move about. There was lots of room outside for Hope to run around and play as she wished as well.

Hope had lots of toys too, especially dolls. Her closet was filled with so many pretty dresses that she never had to wear the same one twice within a month. Then there was her room, it was decorated like it was part of a fairytale.

But Hope didn't care about her room or how much
space she had because she didn't like
where she lived. It wasn't in the country, but it was an
old house surrounded by tons of trees and flowers.
The nearest house was visible, but still a long distance
away. There were only a handful of neighbors, and
none were children. Well, one neighbor had a kid, but it
was a twelve-year old boy, so that still didn't matter.
Hope was only six and she was a girl.

It was summer now, which meant no school. Summer was always the worst time of all for Hope. Summer Vacation meant that Hope wouldn't even see her school friends.

Hope was not happy with not having a little girl to play with nearby. She got lonely being the only kid in the house. Even though Hope lived with her Ma, G-Ma, and cat Tula who were girls, it didn't substitute having a friend her age.

Hope had wished for a long time that a little girl would move in one of the houses that were closest to her. But that just never happened.

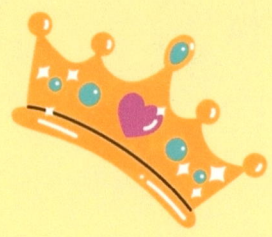

So Hope just pretended that her baby dolls were her friends. She invited them to tea parties, slumber parties, and movie nights. Last summer, Hope had her dolls as guests for her birthday party. She even passed out invitations to them a week ahead of time, so that they'd have time to fit her party into their schedule. This year Hope hoped for a party with real guests.

No doll was a substitution for a real friend who was a real girl. So, Hope decided to wish, and wish, and wish again, for a little girl to move into one of the houses that were closest to her. But that still never happened. The old neighbors never left or moved any little girls in with them.

Hope began to grow unsatisfied with her old dolls. So Ma bought her several new ones. Some were even life-sized But, they still didn't ease Hope's, lonely heart. Hope needed a friend, the type she'd always dreamed of. Hope wanted someone who looked like a real girl and could walk and talk on her own about things that she and Hope shared in common.

One day, Hope was so sad and lonely that she decided not to play at all. She just laid down in her bed and cried. She cried quietly. So, G-Ma and Ma didn't even know that she was crying. Hope cried so long that she cried herself to sleep. But while she was asleep, Hope had a magical dream.

Hope dreamed that she was playing in her sandbox out by her G-ma's flower garden. All of a sudden, a little girl appeared. The little girl had beautiful golden yellow bows and big brown cottony puffs. She was wearing a blue and yellow outfit with sunflowers on it.

"My name is Yanick," said the girl.

"My name is Hope," Hope replied. "Would you like to build a castle in my sandbox?" Hope asked Yanick.

Yanick replied, "I surely would." Then Hope and Yanick began to build.

Hope and Yanick played in the sandbox for a long time. They built the tallest sandcastle that Hope had ever built. This castle was definitely like none that Hope had ever built before because it shimmered and the sand held together, no matter how hard the girls hit it with their shovels.

But what made Hope know that something was special about this sand, was when she and Yanick all of a sudden were inside the castle.
"Wow! Where are we?" the girls asked one another, roaming the long halls of the enchanted castle with amazement.

Hope and Yanick were wearing crowns on their heads and beautiful sparkling gowns. There were two other girls in a large formal dining room, at the end of one of the very long halls of the mysterious castle. These girls were wearing crowns and sparkling gowns as well and were sitting at a long dining table. "Would you like to join us for tea?" the tallest girl asked, holding a golden teacup so sophisticated, like, with her pinky pointing outward.

Hope and Yanick joined the girls for tea and afterward they played a game of hide-and-seek in the royal courtyard. The girls played for hours; it seemed. It was the most fun that Hope had ever had, and a dream come true until-

Hope was awakened by G-ma's voice. "Hope!" G-ma called, standing at the bottom of the stairs. "There's company in the living room," G-ma informed Hope. "Hurry and get down," Mom whispered, popping her head in Hope's doorway.

Hope couldn't imagine who the company could be. They never had company. Their family was scattered across the U.S. and Ma and G-Ma had no friends that just visited.

When Hope came downstairs, she saw a man, woman, and two girls sitting on the living room sofa. The girls looked exactly like the girls who'd invited Hope and Yanick for tea in her dream.

"This is Uncle Jacob and his wife Nadine and their two daughters Kathy and Trudy," G-ma introduced.

"Yes, they moved here from Pennsylvania and will be staying with us for the summer until they find their own place," Ma explained.

"Hope, why don't you take Kathy and Trudy out back to play?" G-ma suggested.

"I packed my tea party set," Trudy said.

Hope couldn't believe what was happening. She was nearly frozen stiff. But she took the girls out back like G-ma suggested.

Kathy and Trudy were around Hope's age, 5 and 8. The girls all played tea party for a long time with dolls and bears as added guests. Hope couldn't believe that her prayer for a friend had finally been answered. She had hoped for a neighbor girl and got two live-in cousins. This was more than she'd ever hoped for.

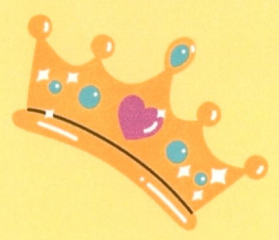

After the three girls finished playing tea party, they played tag and threw the ball for a while. When they were completely worn out, they came around front where they heard their G-ma talking, to ask for some cold lemonade.

G-ma was talking to Mr. and Mrs. Colbert, the neighbors. They were introducing their new adopted daughter to G-ma. The little girl had beautiful golden yellow bows and big brown cottony puffs. She was wearing a blue and yellow outfit with sunflowers on it.

"G-ma, this is Yanick." Mrs. Colbert said proudly.

Yanick waved at Hope and asked, "Do you have a sandbox I can make a giant sand castle."

"Hey, we can all be princesses. I have four princess crowns in my duffle bag," Kathy added.

So the four girls drank their lemonade and went back to the backyard to Hope's sandbox that set near G-ma's flower garden. Hope, Kathy, Trudy, and Yanick played in the sandbox for a very long time.

The four girls built the tallest sandcastle that Hope had ever built. It shimmered in the blazing summer sun and the sand held together no matter how hard the girls hit it with their shovels. This castle was definitely like none that Hope had ever built, except in her dreams.

FAIRYTALE ENDINGS

IMAGINARY FRIENDS

Character Designed by
Schertevear Q.Watkins

Hope

Comprehension Section

Thinking Questions

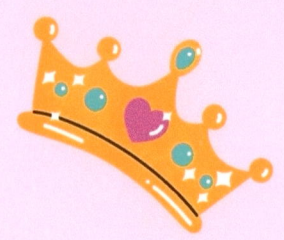

What season do you think was Hope's least favorite?

Why did Hope stare at the house across the street so much?

Hope had lots of toys, clothing, and a big, beautiful room. Why didn't all these things keep her happy?

Why do you think Hope ended up in a magical castle and not a magical forest or a spooky cave?

What was so wonderful about Hope's dream?

Who do you think the children were in Hope's dream?

Recalling The Details

What was Hope's neighborhood like?

Who does Hope invite to her birthday party?

Why doesn't Hope play with the child that lives on her street?

 # More About the Story

What is the name of this book?

Who are the Authors and/or Illustrators?

Who is the main character in this story?

What is the mood of the main character?
Why does she feel this way?

Does this story have a happy ending? Why?

What does the Author want children to learn when
they read or hear this story?

What is your opinion about the main
character's problem and the outcome?

Check out this Book

on

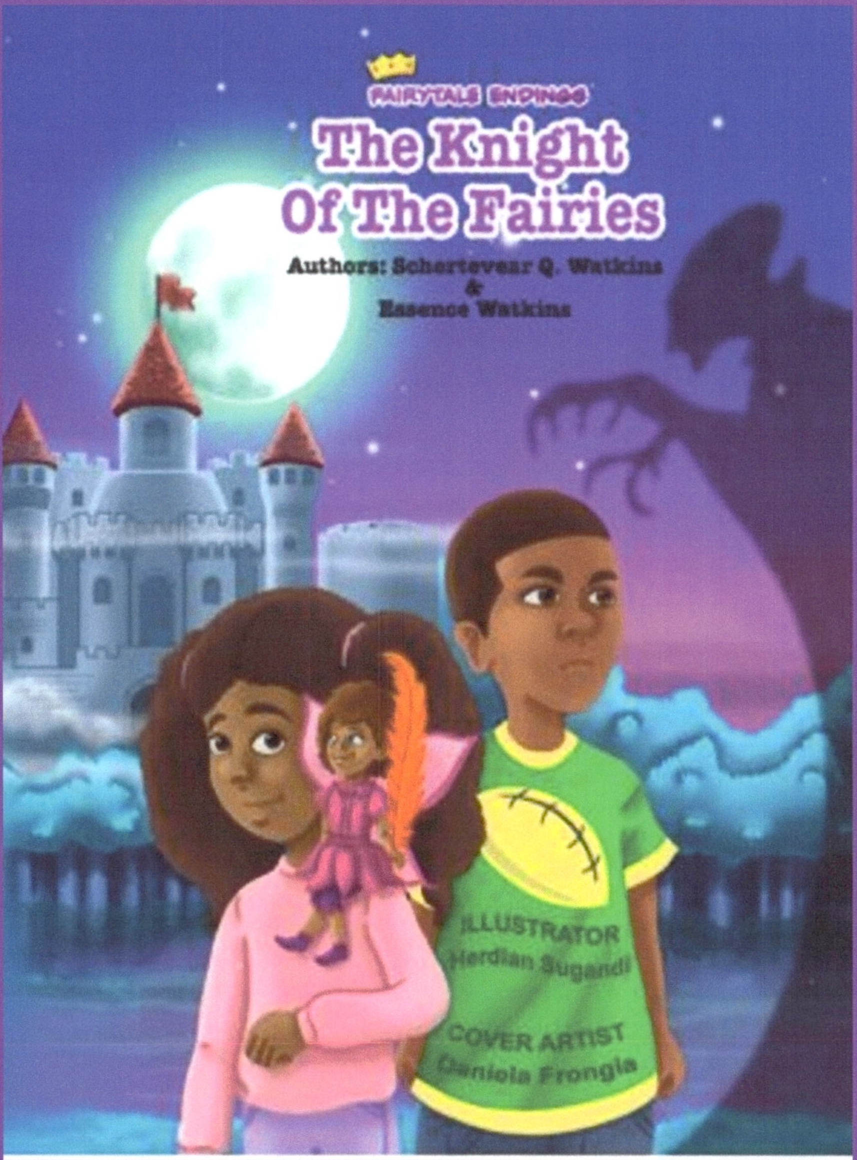

FOLLOW THE AUTHOR.

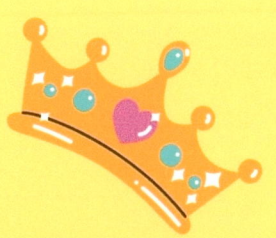

Don't forget to review this Book

on